MY CRAZY SISTER

New York   The Dial Press

MY
CRAZY SISTER

STORIES AND PICTURES BY

M.B. GOFFSTEIN

Library of Congress Cataloging in Publication Data
Goffstein, M B   My Crazy Sister.
Summary: Two sisters live together happily,
but sometimes one does crazy things.
[1. Brothers and sisters—Fiction] I. Title.
PZ7.G5573My   [E]   76-2286
ISBN 0-8037-6198-8   ISBN 0-8037-6199-6 lib. bdg.

To the memory of Melvin Loos,
printer and teacher

MY
CRAZY SISTER

My sister came to live with me
and turned my whole house upside-down.

She drove here in a car
loaded with everything she owned,
her "treasures," she told me.
I said to her, "You are *my* treasure."

After the excitement and confusion
of greeting each other
and bringing her things in from the car,
I put on the table a beautiful dinner,
"like magic," she said,
and we sat down to eat.
We hardly talked during the meal.

Later, with two pink desserts
and two good cups of tea,
for the first time we really looked at each other
and felt our deep joy in being together.

I looked around my room
and saw how her things fit in without crowding.
The car and TV set were large and exciting,
but her other belongings were very small:
a wooden chair, a cradle.
"Sister," I said,
"those things look like they are for a baby."

"My baby!" she cried, staring around.
"You mean you have a baby?"
"I did, I did!" she moaned.
  My crazy sister.

At last we found him high up on my shelf
where she had placed him
between the clock and the vase.
Once he was safely down
and we fed him milk and a little cake,
my sister put him in his cradle.

There he lay calmly and caused no more worry.
What a good baby!
Without my even having to ask her,
my sister helped me clean up the kitchen.

Then we went out to the porch
and sat down on the glider
and watched some television before bed.
We turned a knob, and show people were in the room.
They talked.
We turned a knob, and they were gone.

Now there is such a feeling of happiness inside me
as I lie beside her in the semi-dark,
because there is a light on for the baby
that stays on all night.

MY
CRAZY SISTER
BUYS
A
RAILROAD
CAR

Soon after my sister and her baby
moved into my house with me,
we carried the washtub
in from the porch
and gave the baby a bath.
"Today is his birthday," my sister told me.
"Not really!" I cried.

"What would you like for your birthday?"
  I asked the baby.
"Choo-choo," he said.
  And because it was a special day,
  we put him in the middle of our big bed
  for his nap.
  Then I went to the door with my sister.
"Buy him a train," I whispered.

"I just hope I can find one," she said
    as she got into her car and drove off.

I stayed home in the kitchen,
so even though the baby kept waking up
and I kept telling him,
"Sh-h! Go to sleep,"
by the time my sister came home,
his birthday cake was ready.
"Did you get it?" I whispered.
"Come out here and see," she said.

I went out the door in a hurry.

There stood a railway car in our yard!

"Sister," I said, "I meant a *toy* train."

"Did you?" she asked me.

My crazy sister.

The baby was up again when we came in,
    and we carried his birthday dinner outside.
"Whoo-oo-whooo," said the baby
    when he saw his amazing present.
"Whoo-oo-whooo"—just like a train whistle.

After dinner I had a surprise for my sister.
Back into the house I went
and got my guitar and a banjo
from under the bed.
We put them around our necks
and tapped our toes and sang:

"*Freight train, freight train, goin' so fast,*
  Freight train, freight train, goin' so fast…"
"Whoo-oo-whooo," sang the baby.
"Whoo-oo-whooo-oo-whooo-oo,"
  until it was late,
  and we had to go inside
  and go to bed.

MY
CRAZY SISTER
STEALS
AN
AIRPLANE

To show my sister I was glad
that she and her baby lived here,
I bought her a picture of Amelia Earhart,
the great American woman flier.
She put it right up on the wall.

"Do you think I look like her?"
  she asked me.
"A little bit," I said.
  That night my sister rolled out of bed,
  and the bump woke me up.

"Sister," I asked, "are you all right?"
"A-okay," she called from the floor.
"I just had to make a crash landing."
  I told her she was only dreaming,
  and she got back in bed.
  But the next morning she acted very quiet,
  and soon after breakfast
  I heard her car drive away.

It was late afternoon,
and the baby and I were digging in the garden
when my crazy sister came home
dragging a small plane behind her car.

"Ah-h!" cried the baby.

"He remembers it," my sister said.

"We saw it standing in a cornfield
   the first time we came here.
   Now it's missing a propeller,
   but I'll find one somewhere.
   The pilot shouldn't have abandoned it,"
she added sternly.

Then we all admired the plane's straight wings
and its wheels and slender body
until the sky grew pitch-dark.

Back inside the kitchen with the lights on
I made popcorn in a pan.
Then the baby fell asleep,
and we put him to bed.
But at last we were too tired to go on talking
about the places we would see
when my sister learned to fly her plane.

No sooner had we gone to sleep
than we were both wide awake,
staring at each other under the blankets.

There were loud men's voices in our yard,
  and we heard a great clanging and banging.
"The pilot and his mechanic!" breathed my sister.

In the morning when we went outside,
the little plane was gone.